Positively UPtimistic

Lisa Y. Lomeli
Illustrated by Patrick Joven

Fulton Books, Inc.
Meadville, PA

Published by Fulton Books 2020

ISBN 978-1-64654-569-8 (hardcover)
ISBN 978-1-64654-568-1 (digital)

Printed in the United States of America

My initial book is dedicated to the ones that make my heart soar. Vanessa, Danielle, Dominique and my tiniest love, my granddaughter, Lisa Marie. You are the loves of my life and the reason I remain Positively UPtomistic. I love you with my soul. A special thank you to my husband, Kenneth Carl Ross, also known as Papa Bear. Your love and support in my every endeavor is immensely appreciated. You're the absolute best roomie and best friend. I heart you.

"Good Golly! I'm finally seven today!" Molly shouted as she opened her eyes with a huge smile. "It's my birthday!" Molly lay in bed for just a few moments, allowing herself to bask in the warm sunlight, which caressed her skin and bathed her bright red curly hair and countless freckles. Molly had been looking forward to this day for what seemed an eternity. The number 7 was her favorite, luckiest number of all.

Madeline, Molly's mother, had been planning every detail of Molly's seventh birthday party for months. She assured that every balloon, party favor, plate, and napkin was in Molly's favorite colors: pink, purple, and teal.

The day is finally here, thought Madeline.

As Molly sprang out of bed, she accidentally stepped on one of her skates, flew up into the air, and came down on all fours.

"Ouch!" she screamed. Molly stood up, smoothed out her ruby red hair, examined her throbbing left pinky and right big toe and rubbed them both before she hobbled toward her bedroom door.

Molly immediately said out loud, "I will not let this ruin my day. I will be *positively* UPtimistic!"

As Molly hobbled downstairs toward the kitchen, she heard the phone ring. Her best friend, Holly, was at the other end. Molly's heart sank as Holly told her she was unable to attend her party. Holly had contracted the dreaded chicken pox. Molly was disappointed. She took a deep breath and said out loud, "I will not let this ruin my day. I will be *positively* UPtimistic!"

Thank goodness! A stroke of good luck, she thought as she turned around and saw the big stack of steamy blueberry pancakes on the kitchen table— her favorite! She sat at the table and spread butter and blueberry syrup on her pancakes. She was about to take a bite when she heard a knock at the door.

Madeline opened the door with a smile. She was happy to see the large white box. *Perfect timing*, she thought. Molly knew that her three-tiered birthday cake was in the box. As the driver left their home, Madeline opened the box and gasped. A look of horror spread over her face. They delivered the wrong cake! This cake had green icing with red polka dots and was inscribed, "Happy Birthday, Thomas!" What were they to do? The driver was gone, and there was not enough time before the party began, to correct the problem.

Molly sighed, and although she was clearly disappointed, she smiled and said, "Don't worry, Mom. It's just a cake. I will not allow this to ruin my day. I will be *positively* UPtimistic!"

Molly's guests arrived, and everyone was gathered around the table. Can you believe it? Pete, Molly's pet bullfrog, chose this very moment to dive into the fruit punch bowl and splash Molly's beautiful white party dress.

Molly's dress is ruined! And of course, so is the fruit punch.

Molly managed a grin, shrugged her shoulders, and said, "I will not let this ruin my day, I will be *positively* UPtimistic!"

At that moment, the bell to the front door rang, and all the kids yelled out, "Yay, pizza!"

Ten large boxes of pizza are delivered.

The kids' mouths began to water in anticipation of hot, cheesy, pepperoni pizza, *but*…oh, wait just a minute. This simply cannot be true! *Yuck*! The smell of fish, permeates the room. Every pizza was delivered with anchovies instead of pepperoni. Unbelievable! It's just too much! Molly's UPtimistic attitude reached its peak, and she broke out in a fit of the giggles, followed by uncontrollable laughter. Her guests followed along, including her mother. The anchovies were removed from the pizza, Molly changed into a fresh dress, and the birthday cake turned out scrumptious.

Molly is presented with the most wonderful gifts: friendship, gratitude, and shared laughter. Molly's ability to make the most of a sour situation turned a disaster into a true celebration.

*****

Sometimes things do not turn out as planned, but we always have a choice. We can choose to be negative and grumpy, or we can choose to be *positively* UPtimistic!

Molly had a highly memorable seventh birthday party. Happy birthday, Molly! Oh, and a very happy tenth birthday to Thomas as well.

How will you choose to handle a bull frog in your fruit punch?

About the Author

Lisa Y. Lomeli, lives in Spring, Texas. Positively Uptomistic is Lisa's first published children's book. Her subsequent book, Have you tried Love?, is forthcoming.

CPSIA information can be obtained
at www.ICGtesting.com
Printed in the USA
LVHW012354091120
671140LV00015B/406